Contents

watch us GROW!

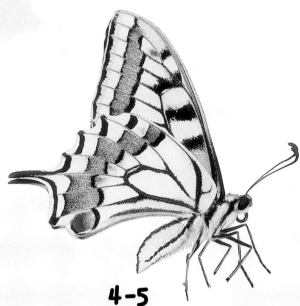

I'm a butterfly

I use my colourful wings to fly from flower to flower, and drink nectar through my long, curly tongue.

Its body is covered with millions of soft hairs.

Antennae help the butterfly to smell and to balance.

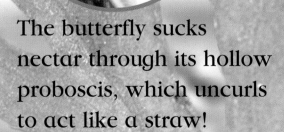

The butterfly sucks nectar through its hollow proboscis, which uncurls to act like a straw!

This is a close-up of my scales.

A butterfly's wings are made up of thousands of tiny scales.

Now turn the page and watch me GROW!...

Before I was born

Mum and dad met while they were flying in a field. They flew around each other for a few minutes, and then landed on a flower to mate.

After mating, the male flies away and the female looks for a plant where she can lay her eggs.

Egg laying

The female curves her bendy body towards a leaf to lay her eggs. The eggs are sticky so they don't roll away.

Home sweet home

Each type of butterfly will lay its eggs on only a few plants. The type of butterfly in this book likes carrot and fennel plants best.

Giant fennel

wild carrot

Time to hatch

After about five days of growing inside my egg, I am ready to hatch out as a tiny caterpillar. I have to chew my way out of my egg. It's hard work.

This two-day-old egg will soon start to change colour.

It takes many hours for the caterpillar to chew its way out of the egg.

Home sweet home
Butterflies live just about anywhere there are flowers. Spring is the best time to find their tiny eggs, but you have to look very carefully.

My eggshell is my first meal!

I am growing bigger

The more I eat, the bigger I get.
Soon, I can't fit into my skin any
more. It's time for me to shed my
old skin and grow a bigger skin.
Each skin is a different colour.

7 days   **12 days**   **18 days**

Danger alert
When the caterpillar senses
danger, this orange scent horn
pops up and gives off a stinky
odour to scare away enemies.

Sometimes the
caterpillar eats
its old skin after
shedding.

Caterpillars do not have lungs. Instead, they breathe through holes in their skin.

I'm very hungry

This three-week-old caterpillar has to eat all the time. It has only a few weeks to store enough energy to change into a butterfly.

These are my teeth!

I don't sleep, I just eat, and eat, and eat.

Sharp spikes warn other animals to stay away.

Munch, crunch!

Caterpillars have lots of feet so they can grip on to branches.

Crunchy facts

🦋 Caterpillars are fussy eaters. Most eat only one or two kinds of plant.

🦋 If you grew as fast as a caterpillar, you would be as big as a truck in two weeks!

13

Holding on tight

After about four weeks I find a nice, strong branch and spin some sticky silk thread to help me hang on. Now I'm ready to shed my skin for the last time.

The pad of coiled thread on my tail is called the pillow.

It's time to begin the change into a butterfly.

The thread around the caterpillar's middle is called the belt.

The caterpillar sheds its skin. Underneath, a shell has formed.

The shell will harden into a protective case called a chrysalis.

Inside, the caterpillar turns into a lump of soft, squidgy jelly.

Time to break out

It's been almost three weeks since I started changing. The soft jelly inside my chrysalis is turning into the body of a beautiful butterfly.

See-through package
When it is time to hatch, the chrysalis turns clear. Look closely. Can you see the colour of the new butterfly?

I **push** and I **shove** and my chrysalis splits open.

When the butterfly emerges, its wings are wet and crumpled.

Hatching facts

🦋 Some butterflies spend the winter in their chrysalis, then hatch in the spring.

🦋 A butterfly's skeleton is on the outside of its body to protect it.

The butterfly pumps blood into its wings to help them expand.

17

Get ready to fly

It only takes a few minutes for my wings to dry off. Now I am ready to look for flowers, which is where I will find my new food.

The empty chrysalis is left behind.

18

My wings are dry and I'm ready to fly.

The adult butterfly
will live for about
a month, so there
is not much time
to find a mate.

Slurp slurp
From now on, the butterfly
will drink nectar through
its tongue, or proboscis.

19

The circle of life goes
round and round

Now you know how I turned
into a beautiful butterfly.

My friends from around the world

To scare off birds, the Peacock Butterfly has spots that look like eyes.

Can you find me?

This Leaf Butterfly hides by looking like a dead leaf.

I'm a Pygmy Butterfly and I'm the smallest!

The Clubtail Butterfly lives in warm, wet rainforests.

I'm the biggest. This pale green

My butterfly friends around the world come in all the colours of the rainbow.

This butterfly from South America is called the 88 Butterfly. Can you see why?

The Blue Morpho Butterfly likes to drink the juice of rotting fruit.

The Malachite Butterfly eats bird droppings!

The Queen Alexandra Butterfly comes from New Guinea.

shape shows my real size.

Butterfly facts

🦋 Monarch Butterflies travel 8,800 km (4,000 miles) each year, from the Great Lakes to the Gulf of Mexico and back.

🦋 There are about 28,000 different types of butterfly.

🦋 A butterfly cannot fly if its body temperature falls below 30° C (86° F).

Glossary

Proboscis
The butterfly uses this part of its body to drink nectar.

Shedding
The caterpillar loses its old skin and grows bigger skin.

Hatching
When the baby caterpillar first comes out of its egg.

Chrysalis
The stage when the caterpillar is changing into a butterfly.

Caterpillar
The second stage of a butterfly's life cycle, after egg.

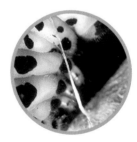

Silk
The thread the caterpillar makes to hold it onto a branch.

Acknowledgments
The publisher would like to thank the following for their kind permission to reproduce their photographs: Jerry Young, Andy Crawford, Frank Greenaway, Colin Keates, Natural History Museum, Derek Hall, Eric Crichton, Kim Taylor, Jane Burton (Key: a=above; c=centre; b=below; l=left; r=right; t=top) 1: Alamy Images t; 2-3: N.H.P.A./Laurie Campbell b; 3: Oxford Scientific Films/Stan Osolinski tr; 4: Duncan McEwan/naturepl.com clb; 4-5: Oxford Scientific Films/Raymond Blythe; 5: Science Photo Library/Andrew Syred tl; 6-7: Flowerphotos/Carol Sharp; 6: Richard Revels; 7: Corbis/George McCarthy (butterfly) ca; 7: Windrush Photos/Richard Revels (leaf & egg) ca; 8-9: FLPA - Images of nature/Ian Rose (background); 8-9: Windrush Photos/Richard Revels c; 9: Woodfall Wild Images/Richard Revels b; 10: Ardea London Ltd/Pascal Goetgheluck clb;

10-11: Oxford Scientific Films/Raymond Blythe; 12-13: FLPA - Images of Nature/Ian Rose (background); 12-13: Hans Christoph Kappel/naturepl.com (caterpillar); 12: N.H.P.A./Daniel Heuclin cra; 14-15: Richard Revels (caterpillar); 15: Richard Revels tr, cr, br; 16: Richard Revels cla, bc; 17: Richard Revels; 18: Richard Revels; 19 Ingo Arndt/naturepl.com r; 20: FLPA - Images of nature/Roger Wilmshurst c; 20: Hans Christoph Kappel/naturepl.com tl; 20: Richard Revels cla, clb, bcl; 21: Sonia Halliday Photographs/Sister Daniel (background); 21: Hans Christoph/naturepl.com c; 24: Ardea London Ltd/Ian Beames br; 24: Oxford Scientific Films/Raymond Blythe tr.

All other images © Dorling Kindersley
For further information see: www.dkimages.com